"Wheeeee!"

WALT DISNEY ANIMATION STUDIOS ARTIST SHOWCASE

Holly's Day at the Pool

Concept and Pictures by **Benson Shum**

Words by **Carol Arrow**

𝒟ISNEY · HYPERION

Los Angeles   New York

When **Piggy Wig** is stuck in a tree,
Holly is the only one who can save him.
Piggy Wig is Dottie's favorite toy.

"Don't worry, Dottie," says Holly.
She lets her imagination run wild.
"I am very brave."

"I agree," says Daddy. . . .

"Now let's go to the pool."

"Pool!"

"Noooooooo!"

"I don't want to go to the pool," says Holly.

"What if . . ."

"The water is too cold?"

"It might be a little cold at first," says Daddy.
"But the longer you stay in the water,
the nicer it will feel."

Then Holly says, "What if . . ."

"Wipe the water away if it gets in your eyes," says Daddy.

"Give a SNORT-SNORT if it gets in your nose.

Shake-shake-shake your head like this if it gets in your ears."

Then Holly says, "What if . . ."

"I sink, sink, sink to the bottom?"

"If you feel yourself sinking, remember your swimming lessons," says Daddy.

"Hold your breath, kick your legs,

and stroke with your arms."

Then Holly says, "What if . . ."

"A **BIG**, scary snapping turtle pinches me?"

"As you can see, Holly," Daddy says,
"there aren't any snapping turtles here.
Ready to make a splash?"

"Splash!"

"No," says Holly.

"What if . . ."

SPLOOSH!

"PIGGY WIG!"

Dottie cries.

"Don't worry," says Holly.
"I'll save Piggy Wig."

Holly **reaches** with her **hand**.

Holly **reaches** with her **foot**.

Holly **holds** her **breath** and **jumps** in.

"Brrrrrrrrrr!"

The water is chilly at first . . .

but soon, it feels nice.

Holly saves Piggy Wig, then she kicks
with her legs and strokes with her arms
all the way to the side of the pool.

Holly wipes the water
from her eyes,

and SNORT-SNORTS
the water from her nose,

and shake-shake-shakes
the water from her ears.

"Here you go,"
says Holly.

"Holly saved Piggy Wig!"
says Dottie.

"You are an excellent swimmer, and a good sister, and a very brave girl," says Daddy.

"I am all of those things," Holly agrees.

"But I am especially brave."

"Except for turtles," says Dottie.

"Aaaaahhh!"

Holly cries, "You're right! And there IS a big, scary snapping turtle in this pool!"

"It's only me," says Bertie.
"We're all playing Pool Tag,
and you're it!"

It turns out Holly is very good
at playing Pool Tag.

And especially . . .

"Daddy, what if . . . I never want to leave?"

"We can always come back tomorrow,"
says Daddy.

"Tomorrow!"

ABOUT WALT DISNEY ANIMATION STUDIOS ARTIST SHOWCASE BOOKS

This series of original picture books puts the spotlight on the incredible artists of Walt Disney Animation Studios.
The pages of each book showcase the personal work of one of these talented artists
and introduce a brand-new world and characters.

For Kaylee, Danek, and Kenzie

First Edition, April 2017

10 9 8 7 6 5 4 3 2 1

FAC-029191-17027

Printed in Malaysia

Text is set in Carnation and Jus Hangin

Designed by Scott Piehl

Illustrations created in Adobe Photoshop

Library of Congress Cataloging-in-Publication Data

Names: Shun, Benson, illustrator.

Title: Holly's day at the pool : a Walt Disney Animation Studios Artist

Showcase / Benson Shun.

Description: Los Angeles ; New York : Disney Hyperion, [2017]

Series: Walt Disney Animation Studios Artist Showcase

Summary: Holly the hippo is fearful about going to the pool with her father and sister,

but when Dottie's toy pig sinks to the bottom, Holly comes to the rescue.

Identifiers: LCCN 2015038430 ISBN 9781484709382

Subjects: CYAC: Swimming-Fiction. Fear-Fiction. Family life-Fiction. Hippopotamus-Fiction.

Classification: LCC PZ7.1.L5178 Hol 2017 | DDC [E]-dc23

LC record available at https://lccn.loc.gov/2015038430

Reinforced binding

Vist www.DisneyBooks.com